POLAR LANDS

BOX 16

Education Library Service

sey

rner

Collins

In the great white North, the long dark lasts all winter and the sun shines on summer nights. This is the tale of a woman who lived there by herself, and was lonely.

The people of the village shared their food with her, so she wasn't hungry. But the woman was sad. She longed for a child of her own.

Often, she walked alone on the icy edge of the shore. One midwinter's day, she saw a scrap of fur shivering and squeaking out on the ice. It was a bear cub.

The cub looked so small and alone on the vast white ice. He didn't try to run away, he was too frozen with cold. He just looked up at her and blinked his big black eyes.

The old woman spoke softly to the bear. "Poor little thing. Come with me." And she carried him home.

Inside her house, the lamp glowed. The old woman held the bear cub close until he was warm. He wriggled and yawned in her arms.

Gently, she rocked him. Softly, she sang to him.

From that day, when the old woman ate, she fed the little bear from her hand.

When she went out, she carried him in her hood, like a child.

And when she slept, the bear cub slept beside her.

He sat at her feet and looked up at her, and she scratched his ears and stroked his soft fur.

Time passed and the cub grew.

Now, his fur was no longer fine and fluffy. It grew thick and silky.

Now, when the old woman went out, the bear skipped and skidded behind her, or tumbled around her feet.

They were happy together. They were a family.

The village children loved the bear, too. They loved playing and rolling and sliding and tumbling with him.

The bear grew fast. He no longer skipped and skidded. Instead, he moved with strong, steady strides.

The people of the village watched the bear as he grew. They saw that his claws had become sharp, that he was strong and powerful. He was too big to play with the children any longer.

Before long, the men called, "Little Bear, come hunting with us. Help us catch salmon and seal!"

Spring arrived and, at last, the days were longer and lighter. By then, the bear had been trained well by the hunters. He could catch salmon and seal himself. Soon, the bear was a better hunter than the men!

When the weather was bad, everyone stayed indoors and shivered. But the bear always went out into the snow and ice. He brought home enough seals for the whole village. The old woman felt proud that her bear provided food for everyone.

But, one day, the hunters returned home earlier than usual. They were shouting for help. The old woman saw her white bear's fur was stained with red. He was injured and the men had to drag him to the old woman's home on a sledge.

"The people living south of here attacked him," the hunters told her. "They want him for his fur and his meat. We helped him escape. He was lucky, this time …"

The children were upset when they saw their friend was hurt, but the adults were worried. Now, the people in the south knew where he lived. A bear of his size could keep a village fed for a long time. What if they came for him again?

The old woman healed the bear's wounds and soon he was well again.
Yet for many days afterwards, the old woman was quiet, thinking.

One evening, the old woman went out walking
alone on the shore. She stood and stared up
at the night sky. One group of stars
blazed brighter than the rest.
They were the stars that made
the shape of a bear. She looked up
at the sky. Perhaps the star bear
would help her decide
what to do.

The next morning, the old woman called the bear to her. She had made a decision. It wasn't safe for him to live in the village any longer. The people from the south might hunt him. They might hurt him.

Her voice creaked with sorrow. "It's time for you to leave, Little Bear."

She put her arms around his neck and hid her face. Her tears ran into his fur. She felt her heart break at the thought of living without him.

"Go." Her voice was a whisper. "Be safe. Be free."

The bear nuzzled his great head against hers for the last time.
He walked slowly out over the ice on silent paws. He looked back
over his shoulder only once. Then he disappeared.

23

The old woman stood looking out into the whiteness. The children of the village came and stood by her. They would miss their friend too, but they understood that it was too dangerous for him to stay. They understood that a bear belongs in the wild. Without a word, they slipped their hands into hers and together, they watched the falling snow cover his tracks for the last time.

When darkness fell, the old woman's neighbours came and led her home. Once more, she was alone.

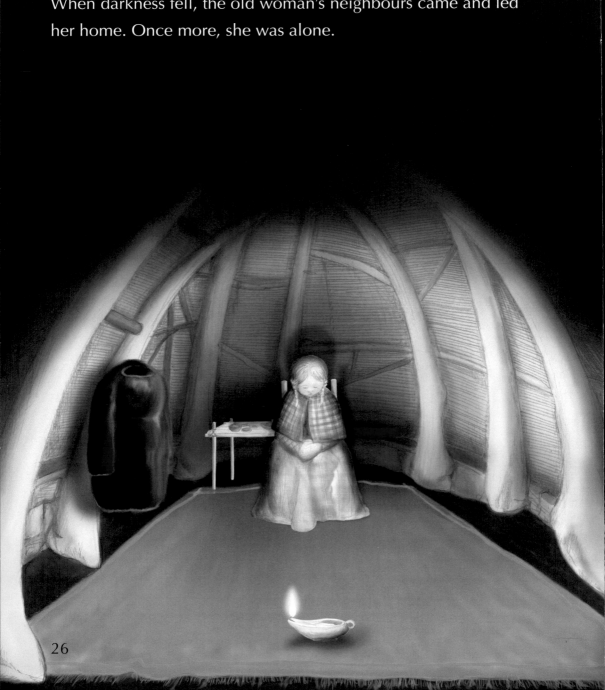

A long time passed. The sea thawed and froze again.

One midwinter's day, the old woman walked far out on to the ice.
She stood there for a long time. The wind whistled and blew snow
around her face. It carried her scent across the wild like a silent shout.

And from out of the whiteness, a sleek, strong bear came to meet her. By setting him free she saved his life and he in turn saved hers.

Now, once a year, in midwinter, the old woman walks out on to the ice. She stands. She waits. And always he comes to her – her little bear.

The old woman and the little bear

loneliness
She longed for a child of her own.

joy
He wriggled and
yawned in her arms.

happiness
And always he comes to her – her little bear.

pride
He brought home
enough seals for the
whole village.

fear
What if they came for him again?

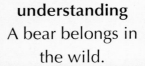

understanding
A bear belongs in
the wild.

loneliness
Once more, she was alone.

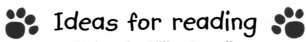

Ideas for reading

Written by Gillian Howell
Primary Literacy Consultant

Learning objectives: *(word reading objectives correspond with White band; all other objectives correspond with Ruby band)* read aloud books closely matched to their improving phonic knowledge, sounding out unfamiliar words accurately, automatically and without undue hesitation; increasing their familiarity with a wide range of books, including fairy stories, myths and legends; drawing inferences such as inferring characters' feelings, thoughts and motives from their actions, and justifying inferences with evidence

Curriculum links: Geography

Interest words: salmon, sledge, decision, whisper, nuzzled, dangerous, neighbours, whistled, scent

Word count: 973

Resources: world map, pens, paper, internet

Getting started

- Look at the cover and read the title together. Discuss the cover illustration and check the children know what the woman is holding.

- Explain that this book is set in Greenland, and ask the children what they know about the country. Locate it on a map and briefly discuss the climate.

- Ask the children what a folktale is and to predict what sort of story this will be.

- Turn to the back cover and read the blurb together. Ask the children what they think might happen in the story, based on the blurb and the cover illustrations. Do they think it will be funny, scary or sad? Ask them to give a reason for their opinion.

Reading and responding

- Ask the children to read the story together. Remind them to use their knowledge of phonics and contextual clues to help them work out new words.

- As they read, pause at significant events, e.g. on p5, ask why the woman took the bear home. How do they think the woman feels? How do they think the bear feels?